THE ADVENTURES OF FRANK AND MUSTARD

Book Publishers Network
P. O. Box 2256
Bothell, WA 98041
425-483-3040
www.bookpublishersnetwork.com

10 9 8 7 6 5 4 3 2 1

Printed in the United States of America

LCCN: 2017944781
ISBN: 978-1-945271-63-2

@FrankMust[a]
The Adventures of Frank and Musta[rd]
The Adventures of Frank and Musta[rd]
FrankandMustard.co[m]

Special Dedication

To my mom, Julie Ann Godden. You have sacrificed your life to make mine worth living. You have supported me in ways that have allowed me to pursue the impossible. You have loved me in ways that I wish everyone could be loved. I am lucky to have you in my life. Thank you for helping me become who I am. I love you!

Executive Producers

Doug and Marie Newport

Editorial Credits

Kristina Oldani, Gary Miranda, Haley Bea

Producer Credits

Julie Godden (Mom), Alex Mondau & Kristina Oldani, A Child's Dream Preschool, The Davidson Family, Elizabeth and Theodore Rose, Jillian Zech, Anna Gustafson, Liam O. Laurie, Canon, Radley, and Addy Neilson, Steve and Annie Butros, Charlie and Nancy Butros, Vicki Hall, Michaela Doelman, Brandon Jacobs, Erik Scott, Dan Rondeau, Myla, Abbygale, Kaden and Scarlet Morrison

Supporter Credits

Kimya Dawson and Panda, Kate Phillips, age 10, Alex Mondau & Kristina Oldani, Kalli and Penny Davidson, Kathy & Rory Irwin, Greya Moskin, A Child's Dream Preschool, Rose Family, The Nash Family, Doug and Marie Newport, Halle and Jacob Gustafson, Amy and Leroy Albano (In Memory of Dorothy), Calan and Lawson Copp, our heroes, Happy Cells Studio, Liz Brown, Kristin Martinez, Skuza Kids, The Kaldor's, Sue Zukowski, Liam O. Laurie, Carter & Eliana Mondau, Jordan D., Neil and Becky Manning, Maya Hicks, Krista and Jayson Kirkwood, The Egan Family, Jeff Brotherton, Jonah Bennett-Cumming, Michaela Doelman

3

Yeah, Frank may be different, but he is DIFFERENTLY AWESOME!

Hey, Lil' Oinky! Do you and your friends want to play kickball with me?

14

23

41

43

45

THE END

1. What did you enjoy most about reading this book?

2. Who is your favorite character? Why?

3. How do you think Frank felt after the kids suggested they didn't want to play with him?

4. Why do you think the kids didn't want to play with Frank?

5. Has someone ever told you they didn't want to play with you? How did you feel?

6. Is it okay to treat someone different because of the way they look? Why or why not?

7. What would you do if you saw someone being mean to someone else because of the way they looked?

8. What makes you Differently Awesome?

Sasquatch Ave

RESTROOMS

Cooper Pants Road

Mud Pie Ave

DIFFERENTLY AWESOME

ASSEMBLY INFORMATION

Awesome Motivational Compelling Inspirational

Perseverance Engaging

Teamwork Courageous

Positive Attitude Leadership Skills Growth Mindset

Adventurous Disability Awareness Educational

After suffering a life changing injury in 2002, Simon Calcavecchia traveled down many different paths until he discovered a life of passion. After overcoming numerous obstacles while dealing with quadriplegia, he discovered his purpose in life by becoming a children's book author and a motivational speaker.

Simon's assembly presentation covers a spectrum of topics such as living with quadriplegia, having a growth mindset, a sense of adventure and persevering through life's challenges. He demonstrates these qualities through videos, music and his compelling story. If you would like Simon to come to your school, then please visit www.FrankandMustard.com.

"It was one of the best assemblies I have ever seen! I have been in education over 25 years, so that says a lot! You are changing lives, Simon... truly changing lives!"
- Principal at Grand Mound Elementary

"Simon was fabulous. He was engaging and inspiring. I would highly recommend him for any assembly!"
- Principal at Boston Harbor Elementary

"Simon was honest, kind, and inspirational. Our students listened and watched in awe as he told his story."
-Teacher at Serendipity Academy

"I think that Simon's message will have a really big impact on the culture of our school and how our students think about disabilities in the future."
-Principal at Marshall Middle School

ABOUT THE ARTIST

Arturo Alvarez was born with a passion to create and has dedicated his life to developing his artistic skills. He studied the Fine Arts at Long Beach Community College, in California. After that, he formed a screen printing business that combined his drawing and graphic design skills. For nine years, Arturo operated a successful screen printing business. The success came from an active approach to collaboration, attendance to community events and assistance to aspiring artists and entrepreneurs.

In 2014, Arturo moved to Washington where he met Simon Calcavecchia. At the time, Simon was leading the construction of a giant Komodo Dragon float that mounted onto his wheelchair for the Procession of the Species. The procession is a parade that takes place in Olympia, Washington every spring. While working on the project together, they became really good friends. They also continued to collaborate on many projects and eventually created The Adventures of Frank and Mustard. This children's book series has created many opportunities for both Arturo and Simon to inspire, educate, and motivate youth throughout the Pacific Northwest.

You can contact Arturo at alvarezarturo31@yahoo.com. To see more of his work check out his Instagram page @your_pencil